A folk tale

Deep in the Woods

Christopher Corr

Frances Lincoln
Children's Books

Deep in the woods
was a little wooden house.
It was painted bright white,
with nine neat windows and a red front door.

It was the perfect little home,
but it stood empty, cold and sad.

One day
a mouse
was passing by
the wooden house.

"This looks like the perfect place
for a little mouse like me," he said to himself,
and scurried inside.

He swept the floors and washed the windows and mopped and wiped
and scoured until everything was squeaky clean.

A frog hopped by
and saw the wooden house,

with its nine neat windows
and red front door.

"This looks like the perfect home!" he said,
and went to see if anyone was in.

"Have you got room
for a handsome frog like me?" he asked,
and the mouse welcomed him
inside to live in the wooden
house together.

A rabbit bounded by
the little wooden house,
with its nine neat windows
and red front door.

She thought it looked like the perfect home,
and so she knocked on the door.

"Have you got room for a pretty rabbit like me?" she asked,
and the mouse and the frog welcomed her inside to live
in the wooden house together.

A beaver bustled past the little
wooden house, with its nine neat
windows and its red
front door…

and so did a fox…

and a rooster, and a deer, and a red squirrel.

"Have you got room for a merry band like us?" they asked,
and the mouse and the frog and the rabbit
welcomed them inside to live in the
wooden house together.

An owl sitting in a tree could see all the animals living together
in the little wooden house with its nine neat windows
and its red front door.

He flew down
and knocked
on the door
with his beak…

…and so did two magpies and a woodpecker!

"Have you got room for some feathered friends like us?"
they asked, and squeezed inside to live with the mouse and the frog
and the rabbit and the beaver and the fox and the rooster
and the deer and the squirrel.

The animals felt very glad to live together
in the little wooden house with its nine neat windows
and its red front door.

"It's the perfect home!" they said.

The animals were so happy all together!

They filled the little wooden house with their singing
and their dancing, and they played into the night.

The animals' music floated through the woods,
and tickled the ears of a big brown bear.

He followed the sound
until he found the little wooden house.
Through each of the nine neat windows he could see a
different creature – each one as happy as could be.

The bear knocked on the red front door.

"Have you got room for a great big bear like me?" he asked.

The music stopped. The dancing ended.
The mouse and the frog and the rabbit and the beaver
and the fox and the rooster and the deer and the squirrel
and the owl and the two magpies and the woodpecker
all came out of the house to meet the bear.
They looked at each other and shook their heads sadly.

"No," they answered unhappily. "There isn't room
for a big bear in this little wooden house!"

"Hmm," said the bear,
"are you sure?"

He tried to get in
through the nine
neat windows…

He tried to get in
through the red
front door…

And last of all,
he climbed up onto
the roof.

The little
wooden house
began to
tremble.

'Crrrreeaaak!'
heard the animals, and they looked nervously up at the great big bear on top of the little wooden house.

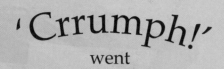
'Crrumph!'
went
the
house.

'Whoomph!'
went
the
bear.

"No!" cried
the animals.

"Oh!" said
the bear.

He dusted himself down.
The little wooden house
had collapsed underneath him.

"Oh no!" sobbed the animals.
"What will we do without our home in the forest?"

Bear felt very sad.
He wished he could think of a way to help.

And then the bear had an idea.

He chopped down trees and
trimmed the branches…

and hammered…

and lifted…

and banged.

The other animals
joined in too.

They
worked and
worked, until…

they had
built a house
that was big enough
for everyone!

It was the perfect home for a mouse and a frog
and a rabbit and a beaver and a fox and a rooster
and a deer and a squirrel and an owl
and two magpies and a woodpecker...
and a bear!

It even had nine neat windows and a red front door.

The only thing left to do now...

was celebrate!